For family
- D.C.

For Ben and his patience
- B.O'D.

My parents
- B.E.

First published in Ireland by Discovery Publications, Brookfield Business Centre,
333 Crumlin Road, Belfast BT14 7EA
Telephone: 028 9049 2410
Email address: declan.carville@ntlworld.com

A CIP catalogue record of this book is available from the British Library.

Printed in Ireland by ColourBooks, Dublin, Ireland

ISBN 0-9538222-4-9

1 2 3 4 5 6 7 8 9 10

The Lost Seagull

Declan Carville
illustrated by Brendan Ellis
book design by Bernard O' Donnell

Brian stood in the bathroom cleaning his teeth. He was trying to remember his spellings - they were getting a test today - but it was proving very difficult with all the noise in the background.
His little sister Mary always played her radio first thing in the morning.

'Accommodation,' he said to himself.
He turned off the water and looked at
himself in the mirror. 'A C C O M ...'
There - he heard it again.
There *was* something outside the window!

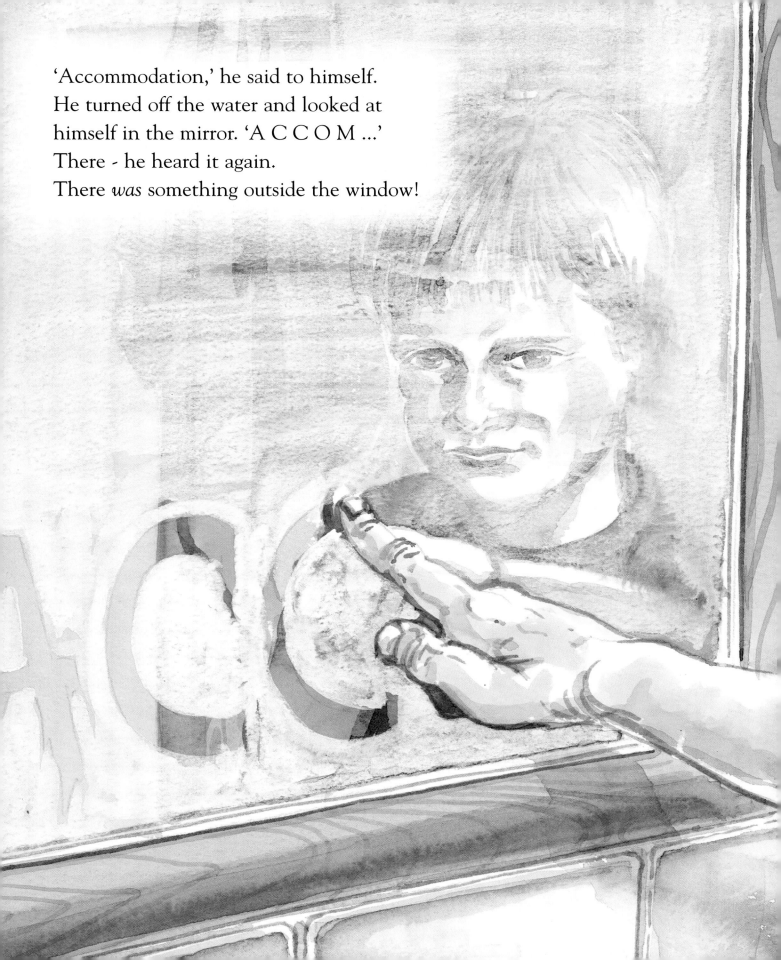

"Mary... turn the music down,"
he shouted at his little sister.
He reached to open the window,
but she made no reply.
He gazed towards the grey sky
outside but he heard nothing.
"What?" shouted Mary from
her bedroom. "What do you want?"
Brian stood silently, but there
was no sound.
He was about to turn away
when - yes! There it was!
He quickly wiped his mouth with
the towel and ran out of the
bathroom, leaping down the stairs.

He met Mary on the staircase.

"What are you shouting about?" she asked him, brushing her hair and looking in the other direction.

"Out of the way," he said, pushing her aside.

He raced past the others in the kitchen, out the back door and stopped.

It was a dull morning. Raining lightly. He stood and listened. After a few minutes he loosened the bolt on the yard door and flung it open wide.

And there it was. A single, grey seagull standing motionless in the alleyway.

For a few moments they just stood and looked at
each other. The seagull didn't seem very interested.
Brian on the other hand couldn't believe his luck.
What a sight! A beautiful bird, standing in their alleyway,
among all the bins and newspapers and old rubbish that
lay scattered around.

"Hello," said Brian eventually.

The bird said nothing. It just stood staring, eyes darting in every direction.

"I heard you. In the bathroom. I was brushing my teeth. Were you here yesterday?" asked Brian.

Still there was no reply.

"Brian," his Dad shouted from the kitchen, "are you ready? We are going soon."
Neither of them moved.
"How long have you been here?" asked Brian again.
"Brian!" his Dad shouted from the kitchen: "We're leaving!"
"I'm lost," replied the bird at last. "I don't know where I am."
"You're in the city," replied Brian. "It's a long way from the sea!"
"The city...?" repeated the bird, gazing around at the mess.

"I love the sea," said Brian, quite excited. "I love to jump in the waves!"
The bird made no reply. Brian could tell it was not very happy.
"I need to get back home. I miss my friends. I miss the sea. This place is so strange..." replied the bird in a low voice.
"It would be great to fly," replied the young boy. "Sometimes I wish I could fly..."
From behind him Brian heard the kitchen door close with a bang and the seagull, startled by the sudden noise, jumped a little in the air.
"Listen," said Brian "I have a plan."

"Can you wait until I come home tonight?" continued the boy. "I've got to go, but promise me you'll wait until I get back."

"I'll be here," replied the bird. "I'm hardly going anywhere…"

"OK. I'll see you tonight." He turned to face the kitchen door but stopped before going back inside. "What's your name by the way?" asked Brian.

"Oisin," replied the seagull, gazing off into the distance. "It sounds like the sea."

School that day was the longest day ever. Brian was sure he had failed his spelling test. He just couldn't concentrate. He counted the hours until it was time to go home. He wondered whether the seagull would still be there. When the bell did eventually ring, he ran all the way back.

As soon as he had reached his house he dropped his bag in the hall and ran straight through the kitchen and out the back door.
"Brian!" his mother exclaimed. "What's the rush? What's going on?"
He didn't have far to go. The seagull was perched on top of the yard wall, gazing down at the young boy.

"Oisin - you're here," he said with relief. A big smile covered Brian's face. He liked the sound of the bird's name. It did sound like the sea. And the ocean as well, he thought. "I was hoping you would still be here. What have you been doing all day? I tried to get home as quickly as I could." The seagull hesitated before replying. "You said you could help me?"

"What a day!" said Brian, leaning up against the yard wall, "I thought it was never going to end. I'm completely out of puff. And we had a test which I'm sure I've failed. I couldn't think straight."

"You said you could help?" interrupted the seagull.

"Oh yes," replied Brian at last. He noticed the seagull was gazing directly at him. "I'm going to the seaside. Well, we all are - at the weekend. You could follow us. You'll meet plenty of your friends there."

"The seaside," repeated the seagull, becoming more alert. "When? Where?"

"Friday. To Killybegs. For the whole weekend. Our hotel has a swimming pool. I can't wait!" said Brian.

"Killybegs," replied the seagull. "Killybegs. I've got an uncle in Killybegs..."

"Then you'll come!" shouted Brian. "Please..."

"Yes, of course I'll come," said the seagull, quite excited at the prospect. "But how far away is Friday? Is there long to wait?"

"The day after tomorrow," replied Brian with a sigh. "Not too long."

"I'm so lonely," replied the seagull. "I just don't belong here."

Oisin looked at Brian. "The wind must have carried me here. It was dark and I lost my way. The others will be worried. I miss my family and my friends so much..." The bird paused for a moment. "But you are very kind. I'm sorry to be so miserable. It's just... I just don't belong in this place."

"You'll be home soon," replied Brian, trying to raise his spirits. "Follow us. We'll get you back."

The next two days dragged, though
Brian had no difficulty getting up in
the morning. Each day he raced into
the bathroom and opened the window.
One morning the seagull was even
perched on the window sill.
They talked every day, several times,
and Brian even tried to give the seagull
some food. The bird had little interest
however. There was only one thing
on its mind.

Oisin was looking forward to following the car. He hadn't been able to fly for quite some time and he was very restless. It was the middle of winter so by the time they left late Friday afternoon it was already dark. Brian sat in the back of the car with Mary.

"What are you looking at?" she asked, catching him staring out the back window.

"Nothing," he replied. But he was looking at Oisin, who was never too far behind.

As it was so dark they didn't drive too fast which made the journey seem long. Brian was sad to be losing the seagull but he knew it was for the best. 'Who ever heard of a seagull living in a backyard?' he thought to himself. 'At least now he will be back with his family and friends. That is the important thing.'

They drove through a lot of little towns with winding streets, full of people trying to get out of the rain. Christmas lights were starting to appear which gave everything a cheerful glow, even though the winter weather was so miserable.

"How far have we to go?" Brian would call out from the back of the car.

"Not long now," his Dad would say.

The seagull flew close to the car the entire journey, but Brian knew himself they were getting near. He could smell the sea.

"Hmme... Do you smell that kids?" said his Mum. "We're almost there."

Suddenly Brian caught sight of Oisin through the sunroof in the car. The seagull was directly overhead. He sat upright, almost wishing he could put his hand out and touch the bird for a last time. 'But I never did get to touch him,' he thought to himself. 'I never even got to stroke his feathers.' Now Brian felt sad. He knew that something was slipping away and that it would never be back again. A seagull, lost in his backyard. It was a chance in a million.

"Would you look at that bird!" interrupted Mary. "It's right above us!"

Their eyes met for a brief moment before the seagull soared away in front of them, leading them into the pretty little town. "Welcome to Killybegs. Ireland's Premier Fishing Port!" his Dad read from the sign as they approached their hotel. Then he started to sing a song.

"Can we go for a swim now Mum?" pleaded Mary, leaning forward in her seat. "Please..."

The next morning everybody was up early. Their hotel bedroom
was beautiful with a large picture window overlooking the busy port.
Mary was barely able to conceal her excitement as she paraded
around the room in her bathing suit, announcing that she was
going for a swim before and after breakfast.
"Slow down young lady," said her Dad. "We have all day you know."
"We're so lucky to have a pool," she said. "Imagine swimming in the
sea at this time of year." Then she started to laugh.

Brian stood gazing out of the window, watching the boats and the seagulls
flying overhead. His Mum came over and put her arm around his shoulder.
"What do you think of this place, Brian?" she said, gazing out at the
water. "How would you like to live here then?"
"It's grand," he replied. "But I wouldn't leave home for anything."

Enjoy more great picture books from Discovery Publications

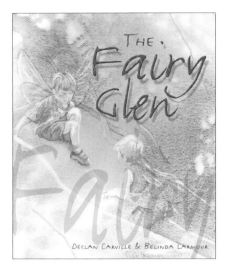

The Fairy Glen

Declan Carville &
Belinda Larmour
ISBN 09538222-3-0

The Incredible Sister Bridget

Declan Carville &
Kieron Black
ISBN 09538222-2-2

A Day to Remember at the Giant's Causeway

Declan Carville &
Brendan Ellis
ISBN 09538222-0-6

Valentine O'Byrne Irish Dancer

Declan Carville &
Brendan Ellis
ISBN 09538222-1-4